ONE MORE DINOSAUR

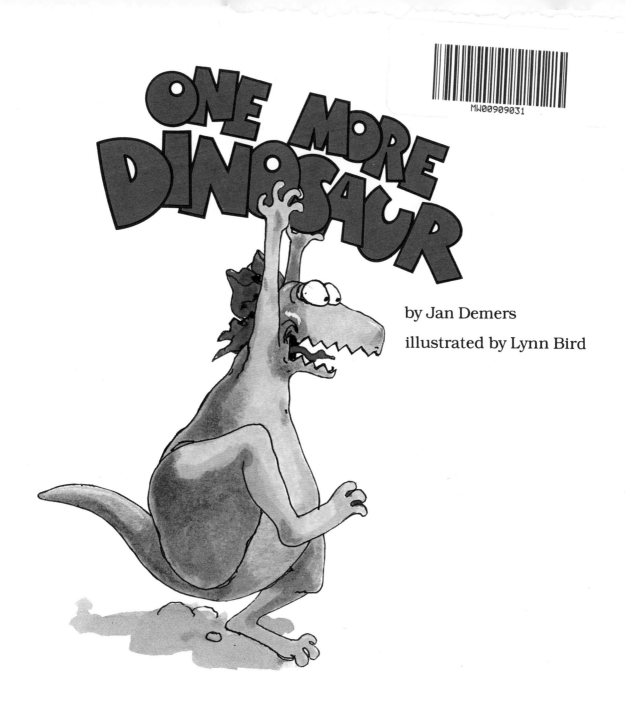

by Jan Demers

illustrated by Lynn Bird

ONE MORE DINOSAUR is one of a series of Predictable Reading Books edited by Dr. Margaret Holland. Books in this series are designed to help young children begin to read naturally and easily. See back cover for additional information.

Published by Willowisp Press, Inc., 401 E. Wilson Bridge Road, Worthington, Ohio 43085

Printed in the United States of America   10 9 8 7 6 5 4 3 2 1   ISBN 0-87406-376-0

One dinosaur in the sun.

Here comes one more dinosaur.
$$1 + 1 = 2$$

Two dinosaurs at the zoo.

Here comes one more dinosau[r]

2 + 1 = 3

Three dinosaurs having tea.

Here comes one more dinosaur.
3 + 1 = 4

Four dinosaurs at the shore.

Here comes one more dinosaur.
4 + 1 = 5

Five dinosaurs like to dive.

Here comes one more dinosaur.
5 + 1 = 6

Six dinosaurs doing kicks.

Here comes one more dinosaur.
6 + 1 = 7

Seven dinosaurs all named Kevin.

Here comes one more dinosaur.
7 + 1 = 8

Eight dinosaurs like to skate.

Here comes one more dinosaur.
8 + 1 = 9

Nine dinosaurs like to climb.

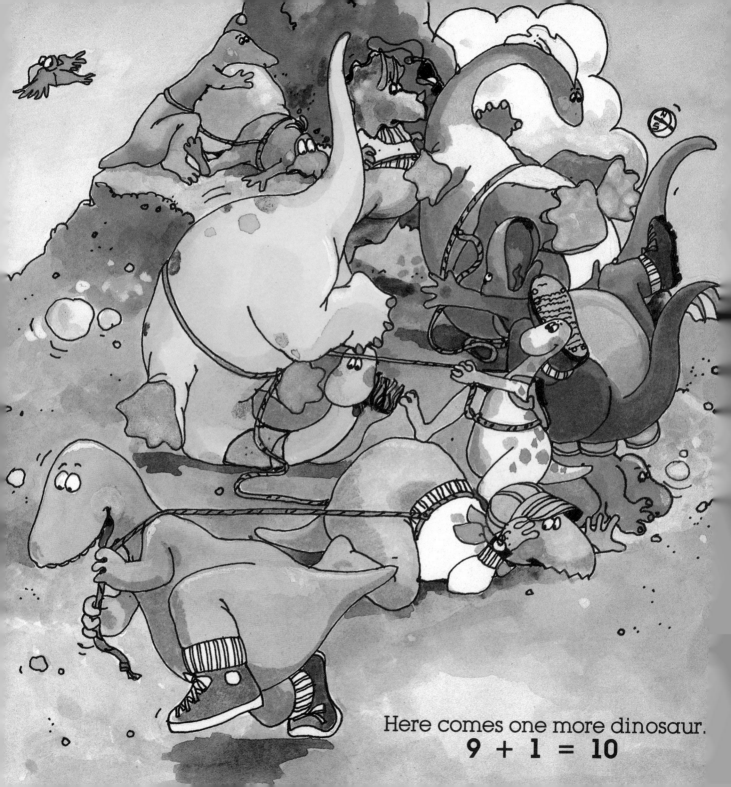

Here comes one more dinosaur.
9 + 1 = 10

Ten dinosaurs hear a roar.

Now there are no dinosaurs.

Made in the USA
Charleston, SC
18 March 2010